I0787943

Beararms McKenzie
and the
Music

A Book By: Will and Katie Baten

Written by: Katie Baten
Illustrations by: Will Baten
Edited by: Caitlin Sattler

Presents

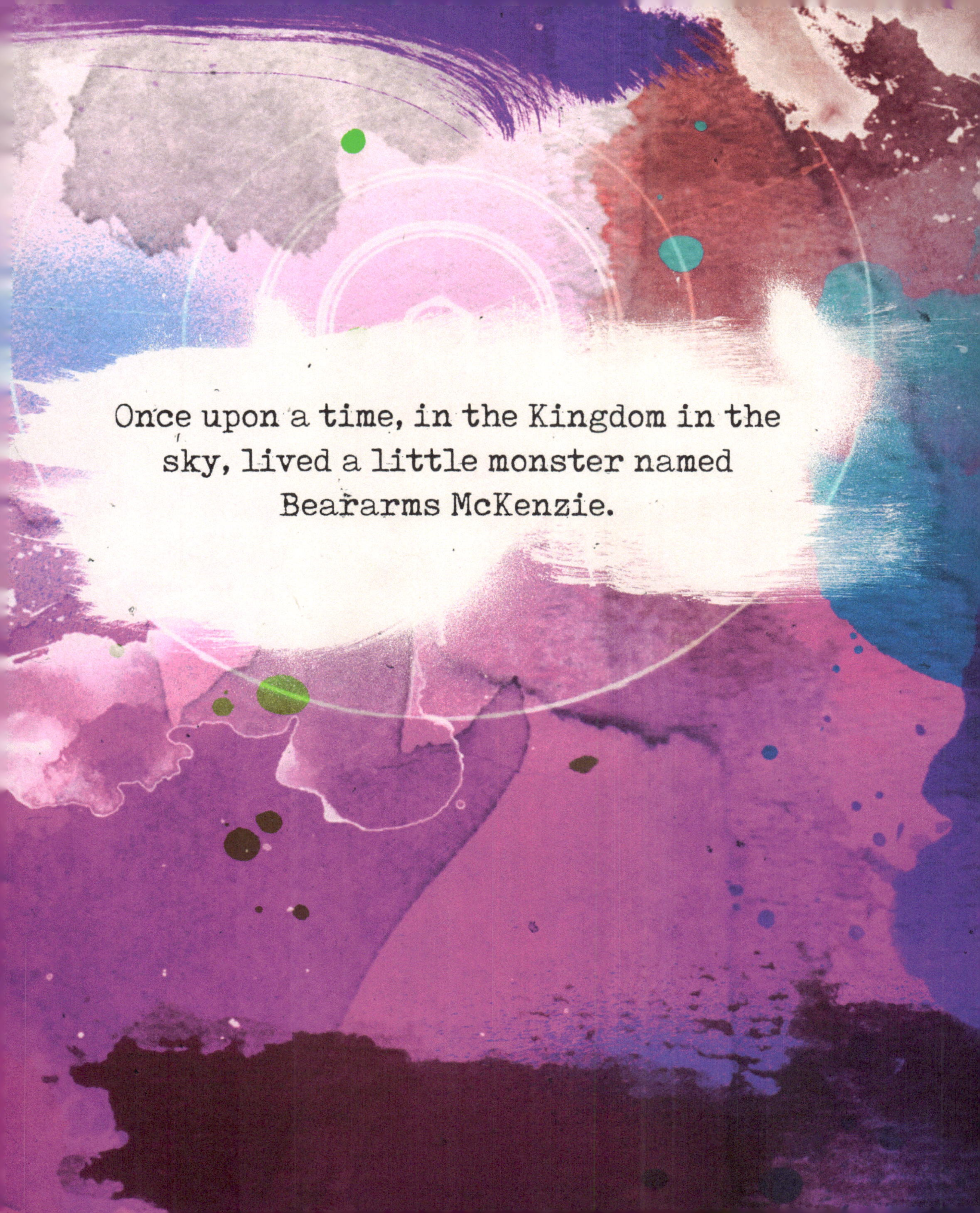

Once upon a time, in the Kingdom in the
sky, lived a little monster named
Beararms McKenzie.

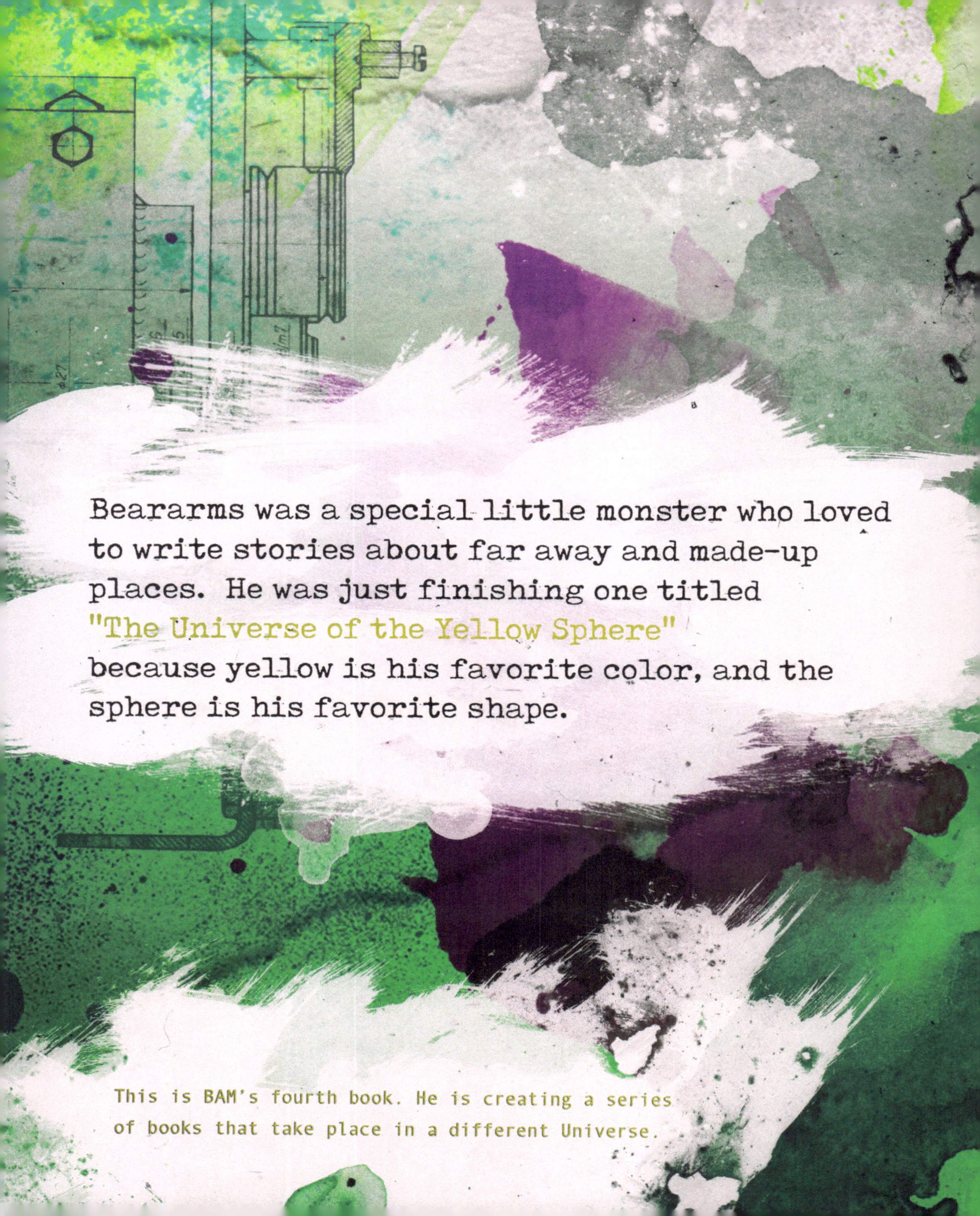

Beararms was a special little monster who loved to write stories about far away and made-up places. He was just finishing one titled "The Universe of the Yellow Sphere" because yellow is his favorite color, and the sphere is his favorite shape.

This is BAM's fourth book. He is creating a series of books that take place in a different Universe.

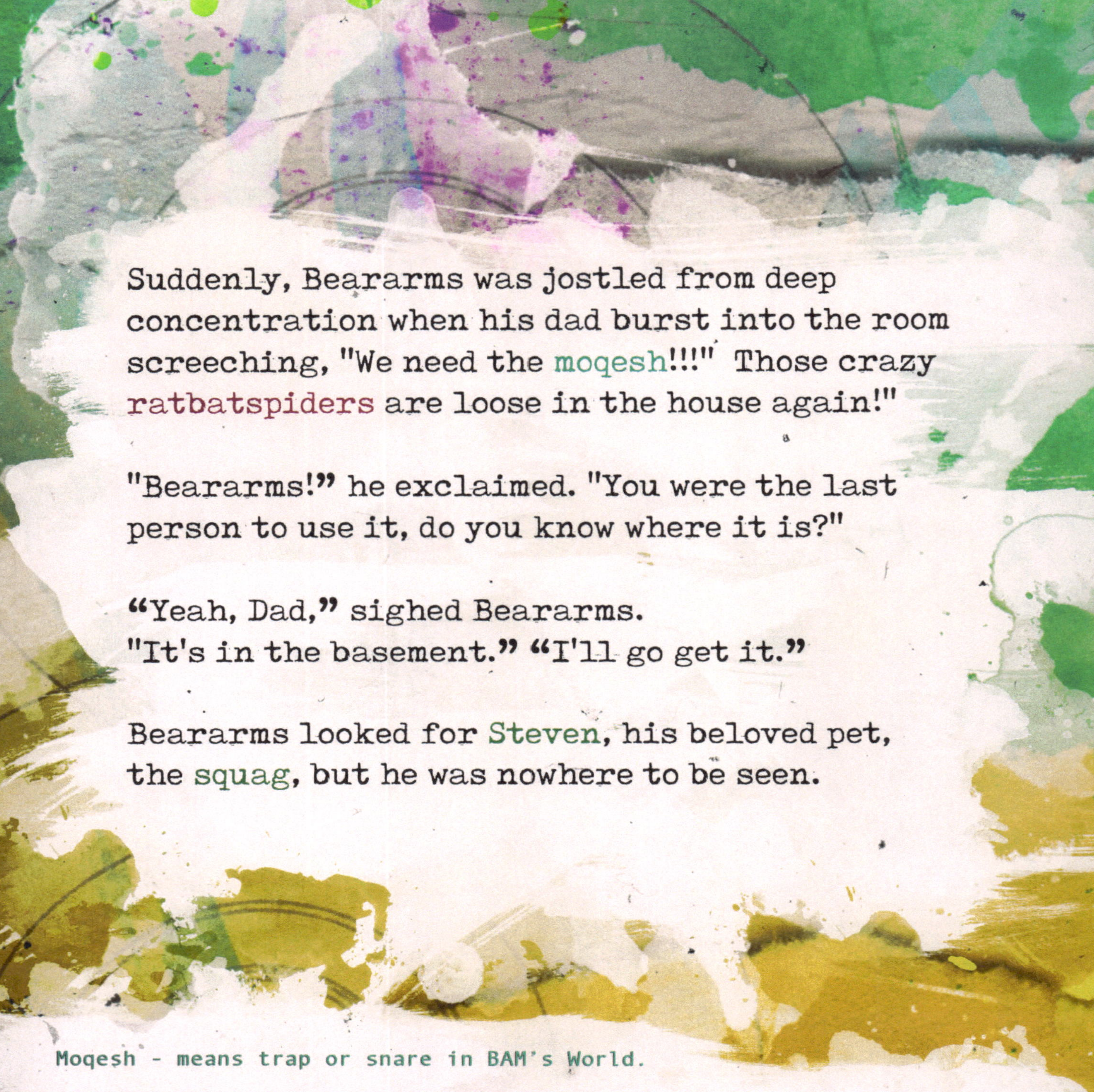

Suddenly, Beararms was jostled from deep concentration when his dad burst into the room screeching, "We need the moqesh!!!!" Those crazy ratbatspiders are loose in the house again!"

"Beararms!" he exclaimed. "You were the last person to use it, do you know where it is?"

"Yeah, Dad," sighed Beararms.
"It's in the basement." "I'll go get it."

Beararms looked for Steven, his beloved pet, the squag, but he was nowhere to be seen.

Moqesh - means trap or snare in BAM's World.

Ratbatspiders are a common nuisance in this World. They are mostly harmless but can quickly become an infestation when food is left on countertops or under your bed. They loved being chased, so they can be hard to catch without a special tool.

Squags are a lot like dogs in our universe. They look a little different, but are still loyal companions. The best way to describe them is a mix between a squirrel and a dog.

upon A time
BiG
on A bike, so she Ran
to the forest....
HUGE Pie"...
one saw
ASHing so
Bears...

Beararms chuckled to himself as he began the descent down the seven flights of stairs
to the basement. "If only Mom would stop leaving bear cheese on the counter,
those ratbatspiders would not be a problem."
Beararms would not admit that he was scared of these harmless creatures,
but he did think they were kind of gross. He did not want his brothers, Pete and Garfunkle,
to find out that he might be scared of anything such as a creepy little animal.

Finally, Beararms made it to the basement.
Some people may have dark or dank basements, but not the McKenzie's.
Beararms actually liked his trips to the basement because he always
knew he would find something fascinating and different each time.

Bear Cheese - A popular snack in BAM's house.

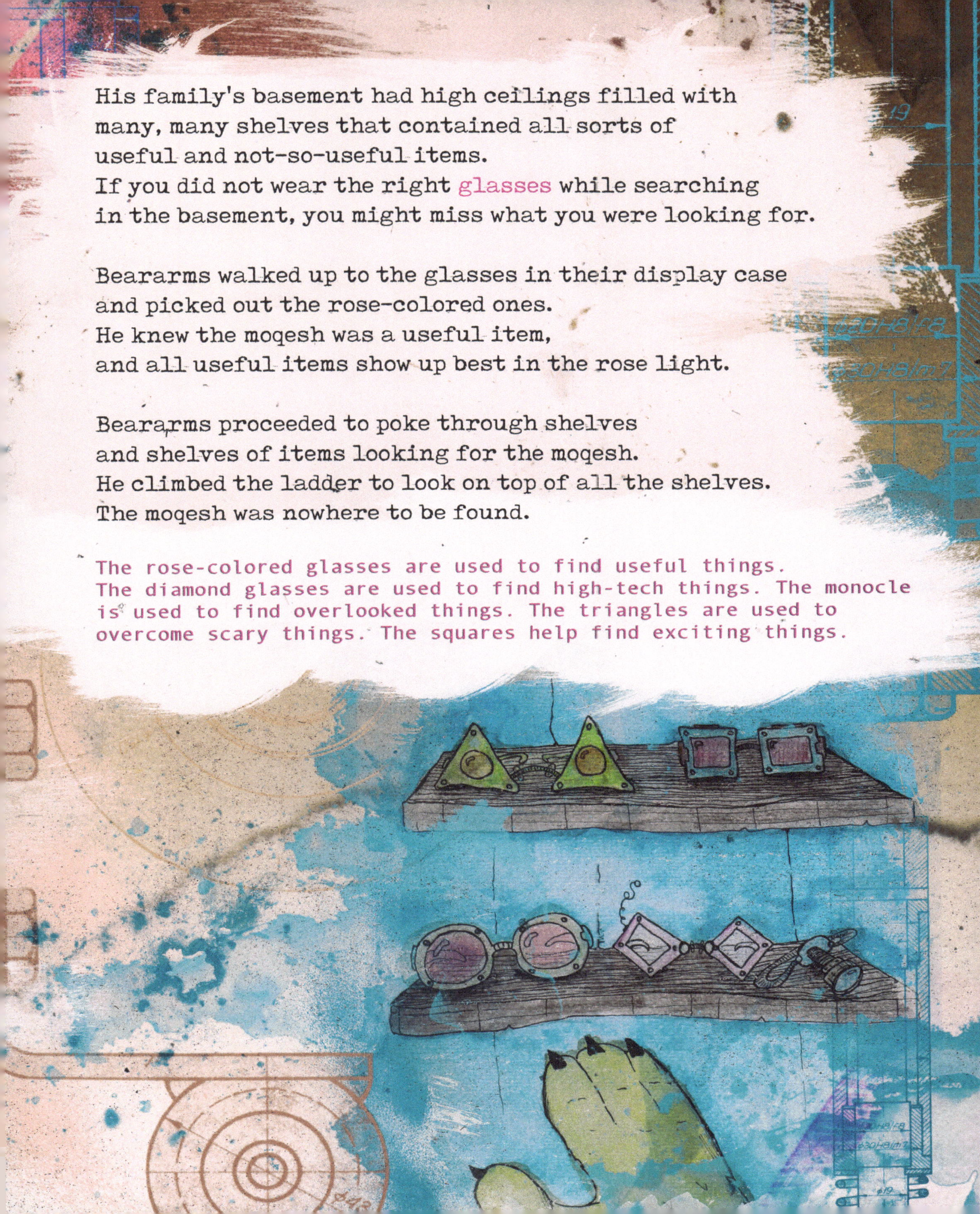

His family's basement had high ceilings filled with
many, many shelves that contained all sorts of
useful and not-so-useful items.
If you did not wear the right glasses while searching
in the basement, you might miss what you were looking for.

Beararms walked up to the glasses in their display case
and picked out the rose-colored ones.
He knew the moqesh was a useful item,
and all useful items show up best in the rose light.

Beararms proceeded to poke through shelves
and shelves of items looking for the moqesh.
He climbed the ladder to look on top of all the shelves.
The moqesh was nowhere to be found.

The rose-colored glasses are used to find useful things.
The diamond glasses are used to find high-tech things. The monocle
is used to find overlooked things. The triangles are used to
overcome scary things. The squares help find exciting things.

Just when he was about to give up,
a bright, green light caught the corner of his eye.
Beararms had never seen such a light in the basement
before so he quickly turned and walked toward it.

As he drew closer, the green light became even more dazzling,
so much so that he had to remove his glasses to get a
good look at the object causing the shimmering glare.

StuF

He found that the light was not really green.
Instead, it was more of a warm, inviting, white,
light. Beararms leaned over to inspect the
object nestled in between old moat decorations
and the hula hoops from last year's hoop-a-thon.

There, just laying on the floor as though
discarded and forgotten forever, was the most
interesting thing Beararms had ever seen.

BAM loves to hoop. Every year he enters the local hoop-a-thon to
raise money for monsters with ratbatspider phobia, commonly known
as chirosurarachnophobia.

The McKenzies are one of the few moat owning families on their home
island. They sometimes decorate the moat for special occasions.

"Dad, dad," called out Beararms as he bounded up the seven flights of stairs to the kitchen. "Here, hand me the moqesh," his dad said absentmindedly as he blindly reached for the object amid the chaos of the ensuing ratbatspider onslaught.

"I couldn't find it," he announced breathlessly, "but I found something so much more interesting." Everyone in the room turned to see what could possibly be more important than catching those irritating ratbatspiders.

Indeed, everyone stopped what they were doing to inspect the intriguingly glowing object held up by Beararms.

Slowly, Dad took the object from his hands and turned it around carefully to view each side. "My goodness," he said cautiously. "I have heard of these devices, but I certainly did not think I would ever see one, let alone in my own house." "What is it, Dad?" asked Beararms.

"Well son, it is an ancient instrument of sorts that was used to discover each person's unique sound. You see, we all have different gifts and talents, but sometimes it is hard to figure out what those are. So in the ancient days, our ancestors used this device to learn what kind of sound they were supposed to make."

"Why is it so important that we play an instrument?" asked Beararms, bewildered.

"In our Kingdom long ago, the King of the Ancient Days found out that many of his subjects were unable to understand what they were to do. Some wanted to be great painters but could not paint, some wanted to be great musicians but could not play, and some wanted to be great writers and mathematicians but did not know how. So he created this instrument to help them find their sound.

You see, Beararms, you take this object and try different keys until you find your sound."

"Do you know what the King of the Ancient Days called it, Dad?" Inquired Beararms. "I'm not sure son, but I think my dad told me that it was once called the Spirit of Light, and when anyone really wanted to know their sound, they would play it, and the Spirit would show them what it was."

BAM's World was a monarchy, with a King and princes and at one time a princess. Times have changed, but the ancient ways are still taught to the young monsters.

Beararms was very curious about the device and decided to get away
from the ruckus in the kitchen to find out if it still worked.

His Dad did not seem overly concerned about it breaking, so
Beararms thought it might be a good idea to see if he could play it.
He carefully turned the device around and around so he could see
all the angles of it. It really was quite marvelous and
entertaining.

Suddenly, it gave off a humming sound, startling the small
monster. Beararms almost threw it on the ground but decided to
turn it over towards the sound instead.

As he followed the vibrations, he noticed one of the panels emitted a
soft, vibrating glow.

"Maybe this is my sound" he thought to himself. Beararms was
unsure as to what to do at this point, but he slowly placed his paw
on the panel to see what would happen.
Almost immediately, the box began to whirl so loudly he thought the
whole house was shaking.

BOOM!!!

At this point, Beararms had all but thrown the device against the wall.
Upon peeking out from behind his closed paw, he saw a
magnificent instrument had taken the place of the device.

Beararms picked it up and turned it over and over. It was a
beautiful stringed instrument constructed with the finest lacquered
wooden body and a lovely, ebony neck.

Beararms remembered his uncle had once taken him to a symphony he had
conducted, and Beararms got to sit close to the pit with all of the
musicians.

Beararms remembered seeing the violinist in the orchestra use a long
bow to strum the strings, and it had made such a beautiful sound. He
stared at the violin for a bit, then decided to pluck one of the strings
with his nail. A note rang out followed by another rumbling. Beararms
set it on the table and backed away again. This time, he heard a POP, and
out of the middle of the violin came a long bow with another string just
like he had seen at the concert.
He was still unsure of how to play, so he carefully held the beautiful
instrument as he remembered the musicians do and drew the bow over the
strings slowly.

Beararms was really not sure what kind of music it produced, but instead of hearing a sound like he expected, he felt a little bit of a shaking and then WHAM! His whole room was engulfed in a deep violet. It was
such a vibrant color that he stopped playing. It seemed to hang in the
atmosphere and tint everything in his room purple, even Steven, who had
decided to join him.

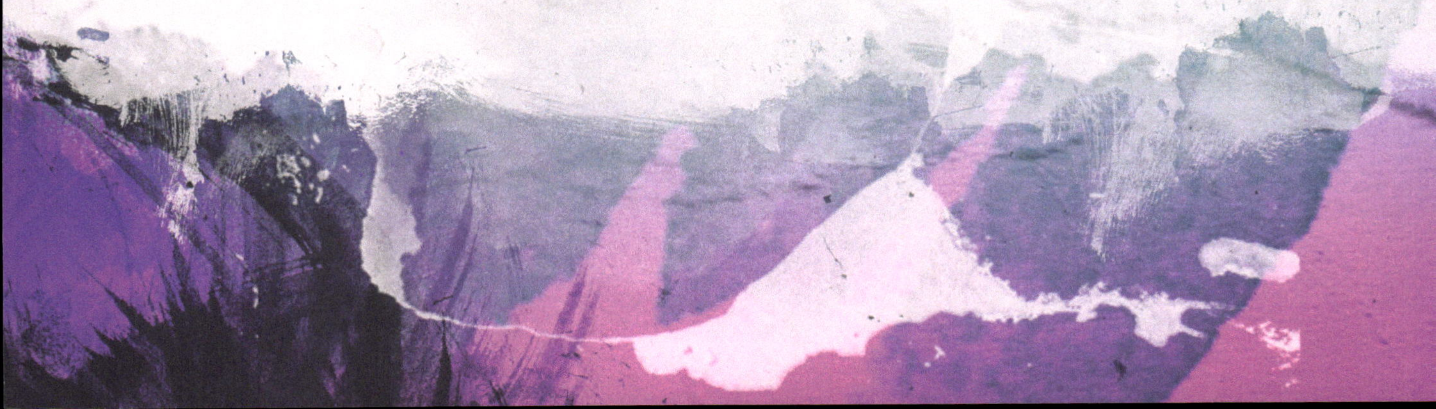

Beararms excitedly picked up the instrument
and continued to play to see what else it would
do. "This must be my color!", he thought excitedly. But something did not feel quite right. He
was not sure what it was, but his hands started
hurting, and something just did not feel right.

Just then, Ragna banged on his door. "STOP IT,
BEARARMS" she screeched. "I'm trying to talk to
my friends, and no one can hear over that awful
racket you are making!"

Beararms stopped and put down the violin. He
knew it took some time to learn to be good at
something new, but Ragna was right. He did feel
like he was making an awful noise.

Ragna is a type of insect that can pick up vibrations and sound faster
than most monsters. If she says something is awful, it probably is.

Upon setting down the instrument, it immediately sucked itself back into the device and was gone from his room. Beararms looked around just to make sure. He was not sure how that was possible, but Dad did say it was an ancient device, so it must be pretty mysterious, as well.

When the device took back the violin, everything in the room was transferred back into its original color, and Beararms' hands were no longer hurt.

I wonder what else is in there, he thought. This time he didn't even have to inspect the device as closely before out of it popped a HUGE, shiny object. It was giant, bright and brassy. I'm not sure about this one, thought Beararms. He tried to remember the orchestra and what was in it, but he just could not picture this one.

I know, thought Beararms. I'll send a picture to my uncle, and he will be able to tell me. So Beararms sent his uncle a picture of the instrument.

"Wow, that is a beautiful tuba!" his uncle responded back. "It is a brass instrument used in the orchestra. Usually we only have one and it makes a very deep sound. It is important to the orchestra because it gives the music its bass."

"How do I play it?" asked Beararms.

"You put your mouth on the mouthpiece to blow and use your paw to play the keys, but you need to sit in a comfortable chair and rest it in your lap. I'm not sure if you'll get it right away because it is very difficult to play it right the first time."

Beararms thought he would give it a try anyway and see what happened.

First, he tried blowing and pressing the keys, but it was much harder than he originally thought. Then, he shifted his paw to see if that would help and relaxed a little bit. This time a long, loud, deep sound burst through room. He was sure someone would come running in to see what happened. It kind of sounded like he sat on a large bulltoadfrog that live in the pond behind the abandoned sewing factory.

He did not see any color this time, so he thought he would give it another try. So he sat there and blew and blew and played his little heart out as much as he could.

BAM uses modern communications similar to our own phones and devices. His world has many striking similarities to our own.

Bulltoadfrogs are quite cute and quite incapable of living on Earth. It takes a fragile ecosystem of water, old string, bits of fabric and the occasional needle to sustain their habitat.

Try as they might monsters are not good sewers. It is mostly due to the size of their paws, hands or tentacles. Either way the sewing factory became abandoned due to lack of use. They now rely on inventions to make their clothes, sheets and other fabric items. The bulltoadfrogs are appreciative.

Nothing was happening. Not a thing. He didn't feel that great about it, but he did not feel very bad, either. Beararms decided to take a look out the window to clear his head.

Beararms was expecting to see the giant redwood tree and the bird's nest that sat right outside of his window, or perhaps the neighbor's dog, Magnolia, trying to dig up old bones in the backyard. Instead what he saw confused and amazed him.

Everything was tinted green! Absolutely everything! And everything was floating. The tree, the cars, the neighbor's house, Magnolia, EVERYTHING.

Wow, what is going on?!?

Just then, Pete and Garfunkel floated by the window. They did not seem to be concerned that they were floating through the air like Winston, the giant green canary that lives in the bell tower downtown, but no, they were just floating along just as green as green can be.

"Hey, Beararms," yelled Pete, "what's wrong with you, did you eat some bad lasagna or something? We heard some really funny sounds coming from your room." Both collapsed into giggles and continued to float around the house.

Well, this certainly does not seem right, thought Beararms.
I do not think the tuba is my sound. Just like that, the tuba was gone, everything returned to its normal color and his brothers
were no longer floating around.

Thankfully, they landed in a pile of grass clippings Magnolia had
ferociously dug up in search of her bones.

Winston is a special bird that is roughly the size of an elephant on
Earth. Canaries live a long time. He is approximately 520 years old and
comes from the Caterpillar Kingdom, which was just too exciting for
him. Winston does not really fly these days; he just floats from place
to place.

These monsters love their bell towers, so the towers are huge and sometimes have inhabitants of local wildlife.

The fuzzy, pint-sized monster began to get a little frustrated and tired of searching for this unknown instrument. This was becoming boring, and he thought he should take a walk.

For one reason or another, he decided to take the device along for the stroll. Together they went down to the Hallmark Hana Falls, a beautiful waterfall in a secluded part of the Kingdom rarely visited. Most people did not want to walk through the Jungle of Ginormous Toadstools to get there, but Beararms did not mind. He found the jungle peaceful and nicely shaded.

Once Beararms reached Hallmark Hana Falls he knew he could relax by a large pool that is deeper than the deepest of the canyons in the Kingdom in the Sky. The small lake is very dark blue and is always churning with foam from the gorgeous green waterfall that pours into it day and night. There is even a little cave he could sit in located directly behind the falls. It is a perfect place to relax and cool off.

The Jungle of the Ginormous Toadstools is abnormally hilly and can be pretty hard to walk through, depending on what type of feet you have. Also, it can become quite windy.

The canyons are not TOO deep, compared to Earth, because the Kingdom is made of mostly floating islands that can attach and detach at will. Still, the waters are a beautiful indigo blue.

Beararms lounged and stared at the pounding waters for awhile just thinking about nothing and enjoying the solitude and small spray from the water's surface.

Then, like an annoyed pet, the box started shaking and nudging his arm. He looked down to see what was happening. But it was not the box that he should have been looking at, for suddenly, PAZOW, he was holding a long, silver cylinder with a hole on top and little buttons at one end.

Here we go again, thought Beararms. He could tell just by holding it that this may not be his sound at all, but he supposed he should try it all the same.

The more he looked at it, Beararms realized he knew exactly which instrument this was: a flute! He remembered seeing an entire flute section in the orchestra pit. They played so beautifully; Beararms recalled the flute having a melancholy, yet comforting sound. He placed his lips near the little hole in the top. He attempted a few notes by pressing the keys and blowing, however, not much happened in the way of spectacular music.

There was another unusual phenomena, though; while he was attempting to play, the waterfall stopped flowing. All of it froze, as if frost had suddenly captured it and held it in place. Beararms became distracted by the solid water and quit trying to play.

WHAM

As soon as he let go of the instrument, the water began its usual roar down the side of the mountain, and the flute was gone just as mysteriously as it had once appeared.

Beararms decided that it was time to head home. He picked up the box and began to make his way through the Jungle of Ginormous Toadstools. It was almost time for the sun to set, and the sky had taken on a gorgeous pink-and-yellow hue. He was very tired from his long day of searching and was very excited to get back to see whether the ratbatspider infestation had been resolved.

Just as he was almost out of the jungle, he spotted a very short toadstool, almost small enough for him to climb on; most of the other toadstools were taller than his castle and quite difficult to climb.

The smaller toadstool was just his height and had something nestled in the center. Beararms drew closer to get a better look. There was a large, round object in the middle with several other smaller round objects around it. Even curiouser were the shiny brass, round objects suspended over the other ones.

Once Beararms got a little closer, he could see that it was a bright, yellow drum set. The drum heads were black, which from a distance, made it stand out a little more. The round, brass objects suspended above it were cymbals.

Beararms knew all about drum sets. His friend, Hand Catchem McGoogoo had a band once. He remembered watching the drummer play wildly onstage. Beararms thought the drums looked fun to play but had never thought of trying before.

Beararms became a little more excited as he climbed onto the toadstool to try out this fantastic drum set. To his surprise, the pedal that went to the biggest drum lit up first, followed by a light on one of the taller drums. He soon realized the device was trying to teach him how to play. He hit each drum head and cymbal in the order the lights appeared.

It was actually easier than he thought. He was sure the music he made sounded better to him than his current audience, a mudskipper that had quickly gone back to its pond upon hearing Beararms play. He was having so much fun he did not care. There was so much excitement he decided to keep playing.

Before long, Beararms realized the entire drum set and Toadstool had turned a very bright yellow. Now, the jungle floor beneath the Toadstool was turning the same color.

This was it! It was a sign! Yellow was Beararms' most favorite color in the entire world, so he surely had just found his sound!

Instead of the instrument disappearing like the others did, the device began to shake like before. The twilight sky in front of Beararms exploded as the box emptied itself of all of its contents.

There was a veritable rainbow of instruments displayed before him. Suddenly, Beararms could see all of the possibilities, but he wanted only one. The yellow drum set that sat before him was his sound.

Mudskippers in BAM's Kingdom are the same as on our planet, except they love music here. If one retreats immediately to the water, you might take it as a subtle hint to stop playing.

Beararms excitedly returned to the castle to see what would happen next. His dad never told him what would happen after he found his sound.

The castle was silent expect for some noise in the backyard. Beararms decided to put the device back in his room before heading outside to see what everyone was doing.

Beararms threw open his door and was about to put the box on the bed when something caught his attention. It was the yellow drum set! It was set up in the corner of his room like it had been there all along.

Beararms walked over to it and inspected it. On one of the drum heads was a little, rolled-up scroll tied with a beautiful, silver ribbon. Beararms gingerly unfolded the scroll. Written at the top of it was the word Instructions.

This must be how you know what to do next, thought Beararms excitedly. He quickly folded down more of the scroll to see what he would do now.

At the bottom of the paper was simply one word: PLAY.

There were no other instructions.

Beararms was confused about what this could mean. He was not even sure if he knew how to play, but he knew one thing that was true: He would certainly try.

It took a while for Beararms to learn to play without everyone covering their ears or leaving the room, but after practice and patience, Beararms was becoming a great drummer. He even joined the band that Hand Catchem had started. Turns out, their drummer had been flying a kite on Mt. Windrush, and the wind blew him right into Caterpillar Kingdom. Everyone knows Catepillar Kingdom is one of the most fun Kingdoms, so they assumed he decided to stay. That, however, is another story for another day.

Oh, by the way, it turned out Steven had hidden the
moqesh in Ragna's bathtub. Which was a relief to
everyone because those crazy ratbatspiders were
now finally under control.

THE END

Our other books!!!! Collect them all!

lunisolarcreativeproductions.com

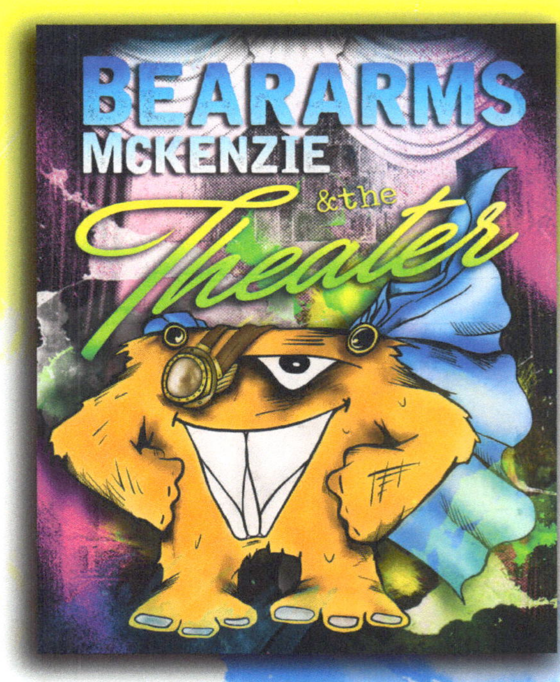